Katie Price's Perfect Ponies

Fancy Dress Ponies

Illustrated by Dynamo Design

Bantam Books

Vicki's Riding School

Vicki

Jess and Rose

Cara and Taffy

Amber and Stella

Sam and Beanz

Mel and Candy

Henrietta and President

Darcy and Duke

Chapter 1

Sam ran into the kitchen, where her big brother Alfie was busy burning toast.

"Mum, where's my wellies?" she shouted.

Sam's mum looked up from her cup of tea. "Where they always are – in the cupboard under the stairs," she said.

Sam dashed over to the cupboard, which was stuffed with bags, boots, shoes, gloves, socks and scarves. After hunting around a bit she went back to the kitchen with a smile on her face.

"Check this out!" she giggled. "I've found a pair but they're different colours."

Alfie took one look at his sister with a red spotty welly on one foot and a blue welly on the other and burst out laughing. "You've lost the plot, you have," he said. "You look like a clown!" He laughed so much he spilled the  milk from his cereal bowl all over the newspaper his dad was trying to read.

Sam's dad shook his head and smiled at his two daft children. "She *is* a clown," he chuckled.

Sam rushed back to the cupboard and poked about a bit more till she found the other blue welly. Running a hand through her spiky ginger hair, she skipped back into the kitchen and grabbed her lunch box.

"Have you got any carrots I can take for Beanz, Mum?"

"That pony gets better fed than me," said Alfie.

Sam grinned at him. "Oh, poor old Alfie. I'll bring you back some bran mash and pony nuts for tea tonight, shall I?" she teased.

Sam's dad was now mopping milk off the paper with his hankie. He looked up. "Calm down, you two. And listen, Sam, just because it's the holidays, don't go mad. We all know how lively you and Beanz can be."

Sam grabbed an apple from the fruit bowl and threw it up in the air. "Beanz wouldn't hurt a fly," she told him.

Her dad looked at her. "I'm serious, Sam. He's a headstrong pony."

"That's why I love him to bits!" Sam said as she dropped the apple and dashed off to find her coat.

Sam ran all the way to Vicki's Riding School with a smile on her face. It was the start of the school holidays, it was a gorgeous day, and she was on her way to see Beanz, the skewbald New Forest pony she was in special charge of. Like her friends at the riding school, Sam couldn't afford a pony of her own. She always worked hard at the yard though.

Sam and her friends, Jess, Amber, Mel and Cara, loved doing all the jobs at the yard. They enjoyed mucking out the stables, cleaning the ponies' tack, grooming them, hosing down the yard and even tidying the muck heap! As a swap, Vicki, the owner of the stables, gave them a free riding lesson every week.

Then, after they'd proved that they were really reliable, she'd given each girl a pony to look after as her own. Vicki had told all the girls that this would mean a lot of hard work for them but they didn't mind.

Vicki had given Sam the responsibility of taking care of Beanz because she had a special relationship with him. Preparing Beanz's feed and watching him stuff his face

made Sam smile with pleasure. He'd stick his
head right into his feed bucket so he could
lick every bit out and then kick it over to
see if there was any food hiding underneath!
Sam loved grooming him too, brushing his
thick coat until it gleamed. And riding him
was fantastic!

It was true that Beanz was frisky, especially
during a jumping lesson. If Sam didn't
concentrate hard, he would rear up and
she'd fall off. But she never moaned. She was
determined to improve her riding and worked

really hard at it. One day she wanted to be good enough to show-jump with Beanz. She had learned a lot from Mel, who was tough and brave and the most talented rider of all the girls. Mel was fearless when she jumped and had a grip of iron – she needed it to handle Candy, the lively Arab she looked after.

Cara, the smallest of Sam's friends at the stables, was nervous about everything – even ponies! Vicki had given her Taffy to look after. Sturdy Taffy was a little palomino Welsh with a creamy blond mane and tail and he had the sweetest nature. He was loyal and laid-back and he wouldn't hurt a fly. Getting to know Taffy had changed Cara's life. He had given her the confidence to start riding and now she was even learning to jump!

Lively Jess, who was the leader of Sam's group, looked after Rose, a graceful and good-natured grey Connemara pony with a stunning silver mane and tail.

Amber, who was the cleverest of the stable girls and the one who always seemed to understand the ponies, had been given gentle Stella to look after. Stella was a black Highland pony with a white blaze.

As Sam came running into the yard, Jess and Amber waved to her.

"Hey!" she called.

Hearing her voice, Beanz popped his head over his stable door and neighed loudly.

Amber's warm dark eyes twinkled. "Beanz wants his breakfast," she said. "He's been calling for you for the last ten minutes, Sam. You're later than usual."

"Yeah," Sam called over her shoulder. "I couldn't find my wellies."

"Not again!" laughed Jess and Amber.

"Coming, babe," shouted Sam, running across to Beanz's stable.

For Sam, opening Beanz's door was the best start to any day. At the sight of her, he neighed softly and moved closer for a cuddle. She stroked his velvety nose and held out a mint on the flat of her hand.

"Who loves you, gorgeous?" she whispered.

Beanz gently lifted his lips and took the mint, tickling Sam's palm as he did so. He crunched noisily while she put on his headcollar and clipped his lead rope to it. She led Beanz outside, where he could enjoy the sunshine while she mucked out his stable.

The ponies were all tied up in a line outside their stables – pretty Rose, gentle Stella, skittish Beanz, spirited little Candy and sturdy Taffy. They, like the girls, were best friends. They all stood together munching their pony nuts and drinking from buckets of cool fresh water.

Inside the stables, the girls chatted to each other as they mucked out. Jess stuck her head over the stall that separated Rose from Beanz, her green eyes twinkling.

"Isn't it great being on holiday?" she said to Sam.

Sam's freckly little nose wrinkled as dust from the hay-net she was filling blew in her face.

"Brilliant! I want to spend every single second here with Beanz," she said.

Amber, whose long shiny black hair was tied up in a ponytail, put her head over the half-open stable door.

"It would be cool to get out and do some shows though," she said. "The ponies will get well fed up stuck in the riding school all summer. And that treasure hunt we did was wicked."

"Good idea! Let's ask Vicki if there are any competitions we can go in for," Sam suggested.

Vicki always inspected the stables after they'd been mucked out. It was a relaxed time when she could chat to the girls and pet the ponies. With her slim figure, thick dark hair, tanned skin and stunning silver-grey eyes, Vicki was living proof that you could be glam and still be a brilliant horsewoman. Last year, when all the girls were new to the yard, Vicki had qualified for Badminton on Jelly, her fabulous Irish-cross thoroughbred. The girls who helped out at the yard completely hero-worshipped Vicki, who worked so hard taking care of her beloved ponies and horses.

The ponies hungrily nudged Vicki's pockets for mints.

"Whoa there, greedy guts," she laughed. She gave each pony a mint, then kissed them

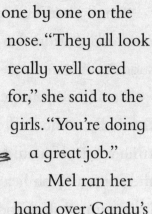

one by one on the nose. "They all look really well cared for," she said to the girls. "You're doing a great job."

Mel ran her hand over Candy's silky chestnut coat and smiled lovingly.

"We've got six whole weeks to spend with them," she said.

Beanz stamped his foot and nudged Sam's bottom with his nose. "I think he wants to go for a roll in the meadow," Sam giggled.

Vicki checked her watch. "Sorry, not yet, the blacksmith will be here in a minute. You'll have to hold the ponies while he shoes them," she said to the girls.

The girls nodded. They all enjoyed watching their ponies get new shoes fitted.

"Who's on the livery rota for this week?" Vicki asked.

Sam and Amber put their hands up.

"Can you two stay with President and Cleopatra while they're being shod then?"

The girls nodded: they knew there was no way that snooty Henrietta Reece-Thomas and Camilla Worthington, who owned President and Cleopatra, would help out when the blacksmith came. Their rich parents paid a lot of money for Vicki and her yard girls to do all the dirty work their little princesses didn't want to do. Henrietta and Camilla would never sink so low as to muck out their ponies' stables or make their feeds! Sam and her friends always felt sorry for President and Cleopatra, who missed out on a lot of love and attention.

It wasn't that Henrietta was ever mean to President, but she never seemed to love and cuddle him. It was a shame, because he was a pony who liked a lot of affection; it made the yard girls sad to see him so unloved.

There was another livery girl at the stables called Darcy, but she wasn't like Camilla and Henrietta. She was rich but not spoiled and she adored Duke, her beautiful dark bay show-jumper. Even though Duke was at livery, Darcy mucked him out whenever she could and made his feeds and filled his hay-net. She enjoyed hanging around with Sam and her friends and they all liked her a lot.

Just before the blacksmith arrived, Sam remembered the question she wanted to ask Vicki. "Are there any summer shows coming up?" she said. "We'd like to take the ponies out somewhere in the holiday."

Vicki nodded. "There's a big show on at Barton next weekend," she said.

Amber, Jess, Mel and Sam grinned excitedly. Cara, who was nervous about anything new, chewed her fingernails.

"Do we have to do something that soon?" she asked anxiously.

Vicki patted her on the arm. "Don't worry, it's a fun show. There are some leaflets on the desk in my office – help yourselves," she said as she ran to open the gate for the blacksmith, who was just driving up in his van.

The girls found the leaflets but they didn't get a chance to read them that morning because they were so busy. The blacksmith was there until lunch time and the girls had a lot to do. They rushed around bringing ponies and horses into the yard, keeping them calm while the shoes were nailed on and then walking them back to their stables.

After the blacksmith had gone, the girls
turned the ponies loose in the pony meadow.
They cantered around wildly, then rolled in
their favourite muddy spot by the stream that
gurgled through the meadow.

Sam shook her head as Beanz covered
himself in mud.

"Sometimes I wonder why I ever bother
grooming him," she grumbled.

Amber gave her a nudge. "Come on,
Moody Bum, let's leave them to play. I'm
starving," she said.

★

16

The girls always left their packed lunches on the old wooden table in the tack room. It was there that they remembered the leaflets they'd stuffed into their pockets. Darcy had arrived to hold Duke while he was being shod. She munched on a sausage roll and peered over Sam's shoulder so she could read the leaflet too.

"Best turned-out rider," Darcy read out loud.

Sam burst out laughing. "Well, that'll be me for sure — not! I had odd wellies on this morning," she said.

"Handy pony competition," was the next suggestion.

Sam shook her head. "No way! Beanz is a handful but he'll never be a handy pony!" she joked.

"Ah, here's a good one: a fancy dress competition," said Amber.

Sam's eyes widened. "Wow! Now that

sounds well good," she said.

Mel quickly swallowed the last of her sandwich so that she could read out loud the details of the fancy dress show. "Hey, there's a prize for best costume and a prize for the funniest costume," she told the others.

Sam was so excited she opened her can of drink too quickly and got sprayed in sticky liquid.

"Fantastic! The funny one is the one for me!" she laughed.

Chapter 2

As the girls sat round the table excitedly discussing the fancy dress competition, the two little stable puppies, Treasure and Hunt, came scampering into the tack room.

"Ruff! Ruff!" they barked in their squeaky voices.

Amber and Cara bent down to pick them up. Cara, who had rescued the puppies from drowning in a millpond, kissed Treasure on her little pink nose.

"Hello, angel," she whispered.

Amber had a real understanding of animals and she settled Hunt, the boy puppy, on her lap.

With a worried expression on her face,
Cara looked up from stroking Treasure. "I've
got no idea what to wear for this fancy dress
show," she said nervously.

Sam smiled at her. "With pretty hair like
yours you should be a fairy," she said.

Cara blushed. "I'd *love* to go as a fairy,"
she said shyly.

Amber, who went to a dance class with
Cara, added, "You could wear your pink
ballet tutu."

"And we've got an old pair of fairy wings in my sister's dressing-up box at home. You could borrow those," Darcy offered.

Cara gasped happily. "Thanks, guys, that'd be great," she said.

Then Sam made them all jump as she got up suddenly and clapped her hands. "Hey, Car – you could dress Taffy up as a unicorn!" she suggested. "All you'd need is a bit of rolled-up card or a plastic cone painted white for a horn."

"That's a wicked idea," Cara said.

As Mel passed her crisps round, she said to Sam, "You've got loads of ideas for Cara but what are you gonna wear for the show?"

Sam was swaying backwards and forwards on two legs of a rickety old chair. She reached out to take a crisp but the chair slipped from underneath her and she went sprawling on the floor. The girls gasped but Sam just lay there laughing her head off.

Seeing that she wasn't hurt, the girls burst
out laughing too.

"Oh, Sam, you're such a clown," giggled
Amber.

Sam scrambled to her feet and grinned.
"That's it, Amber," she said. "You've given me
a cool idea. I'll go to the fancy dress show as
a clown!"

"Wicked!" agreed the others.

Jess twirled her thick brown hair round her
fingers. It was something she did when she
was thinking hard. "D'you think I could go
as Snow White?" she asked.

Mel grinned. "Yeah, but who would be Grumpy?" she joked.

Sam giggled. "Henrietta Toffee-Nose, of course. She'd make a perfect Grumpy!"

No sooner were the words out of her mouth than a shadow fell across the door and snooty Henrietta Reece-Thomas walked into the tack room.

"I hope you aren't going to spend all day eating and gossiping – there's loads of work to be done, you know," she said, looking daggers at Sam and her friends.

Feisty little Mel, who wasn't afraid of anybody, got to her feet. "It's our lunch hour, actually," she snapped.

Treasure and Hunt scampered up to Henrietta and started to nibble her expensive riding boots. Henrietta, who'd been happy to leave the pups when they were drowning, kicked them viciously away.

"Stinking mongrels – you should've left

them to die!" she snapped.

As Cara grabbed the puppies, Mel flew at
Henrietta.

"If you kick them again, I'll kick you
harder," she shouted.

Henrietta glared at her. "Just you try it,"
she said, then, turned and stomped out of the
tack room.

With her dark brown eyes flashing
dangerously, Mel watched Henrietta go.
"What a cow!" she shouted.

Cara, who was gently stroking the pups,

looked up. "Don't worry, Mel, the puppies are fine," she reassured her.

Mel shook her head. She looked worried. "Yeah, but I wouldn't be surprised if one day Henrietta really did hurt Treasure and Hunt," she said.

Sam smiled as she scooped Treasure up into her arms. "We'll just have to keep an eye on Snooty Knickers, won't we, babe?" she said as she tickled the pup's little ears.

Mel burst out laughing. "Snotty Knickers?" she said. "That's the perfect name for her!"

The rest of the afternoon was spent working in the yard and deciding properly what outfits they were going to wear for the fancy dress show.

"We've got to decide what we're wearing, then we can work out what the ponies will need," said Jess.

Sam, who was sweeping the yard with her

and Amber, leaned on her brush. "Well, I'm definitely going as a clown," she said.

"Who's gonna make your costume?" Amber asked.

Sam winked at them. "I've got that sewn up!" she joked. "My mum's brilliant at making clothes."

Jess tipped a wheelbarrow full of horse manure onto the muck heap. "Lucky you," she said. "There's no way my mum's gonna have time to help."

"Don't worry," said Sam. "I'm sure my mum would make something for you too.

Honestly, she loves doing that sort of thing.
And it'll keep her busy and stop her nagging
at me all the time!"

"Really?" said Jess. "Thanks, Sam. You're a
legend!"

"What about you, Amber?" asked Sam.
"Have you made your mind up yet about
what you're going to wear?"

Amber smiled and nodded. "I'm going to
dress up as an Indian princess! I'll wear my
best sari, the one with blue and silver sequins,
and Stella can wear my pink sari under her
saddle and loads of glittery things on her
bridle," she told her.

Sam flicked Amber's long black ponytail.
"What you gonna do with your hair? Wear
it loose under your riding hat?" she asked.

"Yeah," said Amber. "And I'll pin a piece
of sari material round my hat – I'd look
silly in a sari with a hard hat on top," she
laughed.

Sam gave Jess a nudge with her elbow. "Are you still going to the show as Snow White?" she asked.

Jess shook her head. "I've had a better idea. I'm going to dress up as a bride and Rose is going to be my pretty flower pony!"

"That's a really cute idea," said Sam. "Mum'll love making that."

"So Mel and Darcy are the only ones who haven't decided," said Amber.

Sam propped the yard brush up against the fence. "I'm sick of looking at this muck heap," she said. "Let's go and help them make their minds up."

Mel, Darcy and Cara were in the tack room flicking through a pile of old comics. Sam threw a dandy brush at them.

"Don't be so lazy, you lot! We've just swept out the yard," she said.

Cara, Darcy and Mel looked up and grinned sheepishly.

Mel pointed at the comics scattered all over the wooden table. "We've been looking at them to try and get some ideas," she explained.

Darcy's face lit up as she smiled with excitement. "I'm going to dress up as Alice in Wonderland," she told her friends.

"But Alice in Wonderland always wears a blue hairband – how will you manage that with a hard hat?" Sam asked her.

Darcy giggled. "Easy, I'll put a silk over my riding hat and glue a hairband to that," she replied.

Jess nudged Mel. "You're the last one to make your mind up," she said.

Mel winked at her. "I've got a brill idea from one of these comics. I'm going to be a cowgirl," she announced. "And Candy's gonna be my rodeo pony."

She turned round as Treasure and Hunt came scampering into the tack room, followed by Vicki, who was chasing after them with a smile on her face.

"These little terrors keep escaping from my kitchen," she complained.

Mel and Darcy picked up the pups, who licked their fingers. Mel buried her nose in Hunt's warm little neck. "Mmmmm, you smell better than fish and chips," she said.

"We're going in for the fancy dress show," Jess told Vicki. "And we've all decided what we're going to wear."

Vicki looked round at them questioningly. "Well, don't keep me in suspense," she said.

"I'm going as a bride and Amber's dressing up as an Indian princess," Jess said.

"And I'm going as a clown," Sam added.

Vicki smiled at her excited face. "Why

doesn't that surprise me?" she joked.

Cara blushed. "I'm going as a fairy," she said shyly.

"And I'm going as a cowgirl," laughed Mel.

"What about you, Darcy?" asked Vicki.

"Alice in Wonderland," said Darcy.

Vicki's silver-grey eyes widened. "Perfect!" she said. "And who's going to make all these fancy costumes?"

"We are," Jess replied.

Amber smiled. "Well, maybe with a bit of help from our mums," she said.

But suddenly Henrietta and Camilla walked into the room and the happy mood changed. It was clear from the look on Henrietta's face that they'd been listening to the conversation.

"Would anybody like to know what *we're* going to wear?" Henrietta asked snootily.

None of the girls were bothered, but Vicki

nodded and smiled out of politeness.

"Mummy's hired a top designer to make my costume and he says he's going to make me look a million dollars," Henrietta told them with a big smirk on her face. "I don't think your costumes are going to be in the same league, do you?"

The girls looked at each other: trust Henrietta to throw money at the event.

Ignoring Henrietta's gloating expression, Vicki turned to Camilla. "And what are you going to wear?" she asked.

Camilla tossed her fashionable layered, brown hair. "I'm going as a queen," she said, her nose in the air.

Vicki put her hand over her mouth to hide her smile. "I'm sure you'll look lovely," she spluttered, then rushed out of the tack room before she got the giggles.

Chapter 3

It turned out that both Amber and Sam's
mums, who asked the girls to call them
Vida and Ruth, were brilliant dressmakers.
The next morning they arrived at the yard

with their portable sewing machines and loads of old material. They'd agreed to help make costumes for all the girls and they set up their sewing machines in the tack room. The two mums chatted away to each other as they measured the girls, cut out lengths of material and stitched the costumes on their machines. Treasure and Hunt loved all the excitement, and were getting loads of attention in the tack room. They also loved playing with the material that was spread out all over the floor.

"Naughty little thing, you can't have that," said Vida when she caught Hunt nibbling the sequins on Amber's sari.

Sam's mum found Treasure fast asleep on the blue silky material Darcy had bought for her Alice dress. "You can't sleep there, lovey," she said as she put the squeaking pup back in his basket.

As well as doing their jobs around the yard, the girls helped Ruth and Vida as much as they could with the costumes. Jess had found a bridal gown and veil in a charity shop, which Vida turned up to make a gorgeous outfit. Jess sat beside Vida, carefully stitching on a long line of pearl buttons right down the back of the dress.

"I never liked sewing at school but I'm so loving this," she said.

All of a sudden, the wedding dress was tugged out of her hands and Jess looked down to see the little dogs pulling it across the room. She chased after them and grabbed the dress just before they dragged it all the way across the muddy yard!

Mel and her brothers, Kyle and Kalvin, had been looking round the charity shops too. Kyle found a child's cowboy hat, which they'd managed to stretch so it fitted over the top of Mel's riding hat. One afternoon Mel was sitting in the tack room sticking feathers and beads onto it. The finished hat looked fantastic against her thick dark

curly hair. She had also found a frumpy old dress made from fake suede, which Ruth made into a brilliant fringed waistcoat. Mel spent ages stitching beads and feathers to the dangling fringes of the waistcoat and she was disappointed that there wasn't enough material to make matching trousers.

"I could wear my old faded jeans, I s'pose," she said.

Sam's mum nodded. "They'll look good with the waistcoat," she agreed.

But Darcy, who was in the tack room for her Alice in Wonderland costume fitting, had a better idea. "I've got a pair of leather chaps you can wear," she said. "My uncle brought them back from America."

Mel was really pleased. They would finish off her colourful cowgirl outfit brilliantly.

As Amber's mum stitched the Alice in Wonderland dress, Darcy sat beside her, sewing lace onto a pair of old-fashioned bloomers that would go under the dress.

"You'll look like a proper little Victorian girl," Vida chuckled.

Sam's mum made her daughter's clown outfit from pink and blue striped material. As she stitched the yellow ruff round the neck, Sam sewed pink pompoms all down the front of the costume. When it was finished, Sam made up her face like

a clown's and pranced up and down the
tack room in her outfit. She even had a
pointy pink clown hat that went over her
riding hat. The girls and the mums laughed
their heads off as Sam did cartwheels and
somersaults.

"You look amazing!" said Jess.

"You'll definitely win for having the
funniest costume," agreed Cara.

Sam held out a pretty flower that was
pinned to her costume. "Smell this," she said.

Mel leaned over to sniff the flower and Sam blasted her in the face with a jet of water.

Mel screamed as water dripped off her chin. "It's a water pistol!" she laughed.

"Ha-ha! *Joke!*" said Sam.

As they all burst out laughing, Sam ran out to the cloakroom. "Back in a sec," she called.

But while she was out of the room, Henrietta stomped in with a face like thunder. Mel groaned and muttered under her breath, "Here comes Snooty Knickers!"

Henrietta stared in disgust at the pompoms, feathers, lace and beads that were lying all over the floor.

"I thought this was a tack room, not a sweat shop!" she snapped.

Vida and Ruth stared at Henrietta. It was obvious that neither of them had ever been spoken to so rudely. Amber's mum answered first.

"I beg your pardon, young lady," she said in an icy-cold voice.

Henrietta didn't even bat an eyelid. "I hope you have permission to make a mess in here," she said.

Sam's mum glared at her. "Vicki told us to work in here," she said.

The horrible tense atmosphere was broken by Sam, who came bouncing back into the room blowing a trumpet that made rude noises. "What d'you think?" she said.

Henrietta's eyes nearly popped out of her

head when she saw Sam's stunning clown costume. She looked her up and down, then stomped out of the tack room, slamming the door hard behind her.

"What's up with her *now*?" Sam asked.

"Your costume, I think," Amber replied.

Jess nodded. "Yeah, she was well jealous."

"Bet it beats her million-dollar dress," said Mel.

Vida shook her head. "She's the rudest girl I've ever met," she seethed.

Sam's mum was furious too. "How dare she talk to you all as if you were some kind of low-life?" she fumed.

Sam gave her mum a hug. "Cool it, Mum. We're not mates with her," she told her. "She's not worth worrying about."

They had a happy afternoon putting the finishing touches to their costumes. Mel sewed more beads onto her cowgirl waistcoat; Amber wound long silver chains round Stella's bridle; Jess plaited pink silk ribbon round some artificial flowers to make a circlet that would hang around Rose's neck; Cara finished painting the plastic cone that was going to be Taffy's unicorn horn; Darcy glued a blue Alice band onto a white silk that would cover her riding hat, and Sam stitched blue and pink pompoms onto her clown's hat. When they'd all finished, they ran over to the office to show Vicki their outfits. After they'd twirled in front of her, she smiled at them.

"You look amazing!" she said. "You've all worked really hard. But you'd better go and show yourselves off to your ponies. You don't want to walk into their stables on the day of the show and freak them out."

Sam looked down at her shocking-pink outfit and giggled. "I totally hadn't thought of that. Good idea, Vicki. This could come as a bit of a shock to Beanz!"

Wearing their costumes, the girls warily approached their ponies in the stables. The ponies all reacted differently to the strange costumes — except for laid-back Taffy, who didn't even blink when Cara crept up to him with her fairy wings flapping!

Beanz took one look at Sam's painted white face with the big red lips and the huge blue circles she'd painted round her eyes, and immediately shied away.

"Whoa there, boy," Sam said gently.

Hearing her familiar voice calmed Beanz down, and when he smelled the mints that Sam held out to him on the palm of her hand, he soon cheered up.

"It's only me, sweetheart, just clowning around," Sam reassured him.

Beanz neighed softly, then walked up to her and nuzzled his nose against her tummy.

"Good boy," she said as she gave him the mint.

As Beanz crunched noisily on the mint,

Sam walked round him patting and stroking him, familiarizing him with the costume. "Take a good look, boy, because this is what I'll be wearing tomorrow," she said as she gave him another mint.

Sam's mum was standing by the stable door looking nervous. "Is he going to be all right?" she whispered.

Sam nodded firmly and started to undo the poppers that secured the front of the outfit. "He'll be fine," she said.

"Why are you taking it off?" her mum asked.

Sam stepped out of her baggy costume wearing jeans and a T-shirt. "I need to try Beanz's outfit on him so he won't be scared when I dress him in it in the morning. I don't want to get my outfit dirty while I'm sorting him out," she explained.

Sam and her mum left the clown costume hanging over the stall and hurried

over to the tack room. They had no idea
that someone had been listening to their
conversation.

Henrietta watched them go, then sneaked
into Beanz's stable carrying a big bottle
of hoof oil. With an evil grin on her face
she undid the bottle and poured the sticky
oil all over Sam's amazing clown costume.
She smiled as the shocking-pink material
became soaked in gloopy black liquid, then
she slipped the empty bottle into her jeans
pocket and crept away.

Chapter 4

Sam grabbed Beanz's colourful spotty pink throw and ran out of the tack room.

Amber chased after her. "Hold on, Sam. I'll come with you," she said.

"What did Stella think of your sari?" asked Sam as they walked across the yard.

"She was pretty cool about it actually," said Amber. "What about Beanz?"

"He really freaked out at first," said Sam.

"Trust you to pick something flashy," Amber teased.

Sam nudged her with her elbow. "We can't all go as gorgeous Indian princesses," she laughed.

But when they opened Beanz's door and saw the clown costume covered in thick black oil, Sam's smile soon faded. She gasped and grabbed Amber's arm.

"I don't believe it — I only left the stable a couple of minutes ago and everything was fine," she cried.

Sam stared in horror at her ruined outfit. Amber picked it up and immediately smelled something she recognized.

"Somebody's poured hoof oil all over it," she said.

Sam burst into tears, leaving big blotches on her clown make-up.

"Don't cry," said Amber. "Please don't cry. We'll sort something."

"But who would do such an evil thing?" Sam sobbed.

The minute the words were out of her mouth Sam knew the answer and so did Amber. They looked at each other and said together, "*Henrietta*!"

Sam grabbed her ruined costume and, before Amber could stop her, she ran to the door. "I'm gonna kill her!" she screamed.

With Amber right behind her, Sam ran over to President's stable, where she

found Henrietta laughing with Camilla
Worthington. Sam threw open the door and
barged in.

"You cow!" she yelled. "You total cow!
How dare you do this!"

Henrietta shook her smart bobbed hair.
"Get out of here!" she sneered.

Sam threw the outfit into her snooty face.
"You've totally ruined my costume!" she
shouted.

"I don't know what you're talking
about but my father could sue you for that
remark!" Henrietta shouted back.

Camilla smirked. "How do you know it
was Henrietta? It could have been one of
your stupid friends," she told them. "They're
all pretty hopeless and clumsy."

At that moment Sam spotted the bottle
poking out of Henrietta's jeans pocket.
She leaned forward and grabbed it before
Henrietta could stop her. Waving the empty

bottle in front of Henrietta's shocked face, Sam yelled, "So why's it empty, eh?"

Henrietta turned bright red and threw the clown costume back at Sam.

Sam ducked to avoid it, but unfortunately it landed on President, who whinnied nervously, then reared up.

"Watch out, Sam!" Amber cried.

But Sam had her back to President and his front hooves were pawing the air just above her head.

"Get out of the way!" Amber yelled. Without thinking of her own safety, she dashed forward to grab President's headcollar, but one of his hooves caught her right arm as he dropped down to the ground.

Her scream of pain brought everybody running from the tack room. By the time they arrived, Amber was lying on the ground. She was white with shock and clearly in a lot of pain. Seeing her mum, she burst into tears.

"Oh, Mum, it hurts so much," she cried.

As Vida fell to her knees to examine her daughter's arm, Vicki came running into the stable and Henrietta and Camilla sneaked out.

"What's happened?" Vicki gasped.

Vida turned to her. "Amber's hurt," she said. "We've got to get her to the hospital now!"

"I've got my car here," offered Sam's mum.

"I'll take you down to casualty."

"Thanks," said Vida, and Amber tried to smile.

"I'll come too," said Sam.

"I don't think we all need to go, sweetie," said her mum.

"But I'll cheer Amber up," insisted Sam. "I'm supposed to be a clown."

"Please let her come," said Amber.

Vicki threw her hands up in the air.

"Will someone *please* tell me what's been happening in here?"

So Sam told her about the costume and the hoof oil and how President had got scared.

"And where's Henrietta now?" asked Vicki, but no one had seen her leave.

As soon as Sam and her mum drove off with Amber and Vida, Cara started to cry. "Poor Amber," she sobbed. "Do you think she's broken her arm?"

"It definitely looks like it," said Vicki. "Jess, turn President out into the meadow – he's probably in a bit of a state after all that commotion. I'm going to look for Henrietta."

With her pretty face set like thunder, she stormed across the yard and caught Henrietta trying to sneak off down the drive.

"I want a word with you in my office now!" Vicki shouted.

Jess, Amber, Cara and Mel would've loved to hear what went on in Vicki's office, but none of them dared creep up and listen. Instead the girls looked after President and then stayed in the tack room so they could stare out of the window. They were all in a state of shock but showed it in different ways. Mel seethed with anger; Cara cried; Darcy kept shaking her head and muttering, "I just can't believe it!"

And Jess was just livid. "I hope Vicki throws Henrietta out," she fumed. "She's gone too far this time."

Cara wiped her eyes with her soggy tissues. "What about poor President?" she sobbed.

Mel paced the tack room with her fists clenched. "I feel so sorry for that pony – he's such a lovely boy. How horrible for him to have Henrietta as his owner!"

Darcy glanced out of the window and saw the office door open.

"Here she comes," she whispered.

All the girls crowded round the window and watched Henrietta stomp across the yard.

"She definitely doesn't look as pleased with herself as she did before," said Mel.

"I hope Vicki really had a go at her," said Jess.

Darcy looked worried. "Henrietta's put Vicki in a really tricky position. If Amber's accident is reported, Vicki could be held responsible," she told them.

Cara's pale blue eyes grew bigger than ever. "But it wasn't *her* fault. She wasn't even *there*," she gasped.

Darcy nodded. "Yeah, but it happened on Vicki's property where she's in charge of everything that goes on," she replied.

Five minutes later Henrietta's grumpy dad roared into the yard in his flash four-wheel drive. He spoke to Henrietta and then they barged into Vicki's office. But he quickly came out looking embarrassed with his daughter. Slamming the door of his massive car, he roared away up the drive with Henrietta.

At the hospital, Amber had an x-ray and the doctor told her that she had two breaks in her left arm.

"They're nasty breaks and we'll have to put your arm in a cast. You'll have to stay in overnight," she told Amber and her mum.

"What about my pony?" asked Amber. "When can I ride again?"

"Not for some time," said the doctor.

"Who's going to look after Stella?" said Amber and she began to sob.

"Don't worry about that," her mum said. "I'm sure your friends will help out."

Sam and her mum went to see Amber on the ward before they left the hospital. Sam started to cry when she saw her friend's arm in a sling.

"It's all my fault. I shouldn't have argued with Henrietta in front of the ponies."

"It wasn't your fault," said Amber sleepily. She'd been given some painkillers and her

arm wasn't hurting as much now. "It's totally Henrietta's fault. I'm going to miss the fancy dress show and I won't be able to ride for ages, the doctor said."

"I know," said Sam. "Your mum told me. You poor thing. You looked so gorgeous in your costume. You'd have won the competition."

"Doesn't matter," murmured Amber. She paused to take a sip of water from the glass on her bedside table. As her mum settled her back on the pillows, Amber looked at Sam.

"I want *you* to wear my costume tomorrow," she told her.

Sam shook her head. "No!" she answered in a shocked voice. "I couldn't do that."

Amber gave a little smile. "Well, I won't be using it and you haven't got a new costume, so why waste it?" she said.

Sam took hold of her friend's free hand and squeezed it gently. "You're so kind but I won't look anywhere near as pretty as you did."

"Course you will. Let's not waste all Mum's hard work and let Henrietta think she's won."

"OK," whispered Sam. "Thanks so much."

Amber squeezed Sam's hand, then fell into a deep sleep.

Chapter 5

The day of the fancy dress show dawned but none of the girls were looking forward to it any more. Sam arrived at the stables to find Jess, Mel, Darcy and Cara looking after Stella, who was very confused. She snuffled each girl in turn and neighed when she realized that none of them was the girl she most wanted to see.

"Oh no. She's really missing Amber," said Jess.

Cara looked upset. "It'll be worse when we all leave and Stella's here on her own."

Mel looked thoughtful. "We could put her in the pony meadow with Dumpling and Flora," she suggested.

Darcy's face lit up and she nodded. "Good idea – those two naughty little ponies will keep her busy all afternoon," she said.

After they'd turned Stella loose, they tried on their outfits in the tack room. There was no laughing like the day before, and certainly no jokes. Sam had texted her friends from the hospital and Amber's mum had been in touch with Vicki, so everybody knew that Amber had broken her arm and was out of action. What they didn't know was Sam's plan to use Amber's beautiful costume, so when she draped the blue sequinned sari around her waist, Mel, Jess, Darcy and Cara stared at her in shock.

"What are you doing with Amber's costume?" Jess asked.

Sam grinned at her friends' surprised faces. "Amber told me to wear it today. I haven't got a costume now and she can't wear this one, so she said I shouldn't let it go to waste," she told them.

Cara's big blue eyes filled with tears.

"Amber's so kind," she said in a wobbly voice.

Sam nodded and nearly cried too. "We all know Henrietta did a horrible thing but we've got to go to the show fighting, for Amber's sake," she said.

Mel agreed. "You're right, Sam. Let's do it for Amber!"

A few minutes later Vicki arrived to check that the girls' costumes would be safe when they got on the ponies. She smiled as she saw the five girls struggling into their outfits

"I've just had a phone call from Vida. Amber's had a good night and will be allowed home this morning," she said.

The girls jumped up and down and waved their arms in the air. "Yessssss!" they yelled.

Vicki held up a hand. "Hold on, there's more. If Amber's strong enough, she's going to come down and watch the show this afternoon."

Vicki clamped her hands over her ears as Jess, Mel, Cara, Darcy and Sam screamed excitedly.

The girls had instantly gone from feeling miserable to being really happy. The thought of Amber being at the show, even if it was only to watch, really cheered them up. They were smiling as they lined up for Vicki to check their outfits.

"Your veil needs to be hooked up a bit more, Jess – I don't want Rose's legs getting tangled up in it," she said.

She examined the posies that Jess had made for Rose. There was a big circle of pink ribbon and wild flowers to go round Rose's silvery-grey neck and a little crown of pink roses that Jess wanted to put on top of Rose's head.

"I've tried tying it on but it keeps falling off," Jess said.

"Don't worry, we can make a knot in Rose's mane, then you can pin the crown to that," Vicki told her.

Cara looked really pretty in her dancing tights and pink tutu with little pink wings attached. Her riding hat was covered in a pink silk and she had a twinkling fairy crown glued to the top of it.

"You look gorgeous!" said Vicki.

Cara blushed with pleasure. "I was going

to dress Taffy up as a unicorn but I've got the same problem as Jess. I don't know how to make the horn stay on his head!"

Vicki laughed. "We can't have a unicorn without a horn! I'll show you what to do before you leave for the show," she offered.

Mel looked cool in her cowgirl outfit with its fringed and beaded waistcoat and blue jeans with Darcy's leather chaps.

"I love your cowboy boots," Vicki said.

Mel grinned. "My brother Kyle found them in a jumble sale. They're too big for me so he stuffed socks in the end of them both and now they fit perfectly!"

Normally Darcy had her straight brown hair in a long plait, but today she wore it loose and it looked gorgeous spilling over her pretty blue dress.

But it was Sam who took Vicki's breath away. She gasped when she saw her in Amber's sari.

"You look totally stunning! Amber will be dead proud of you, Sam," she told her.

When Vicki had inspected the girls' costumes, they changed back into their riding clothes and joined her to check the fancy dress throws the ponies would be wearing under their saddles. Rose had a short white lacy veil, Candy had a striped blanket decorated with beads and feathers, Taffy had a pretty pink blanket, Duke's throw was pale blue trimmed with silver ribbon and Beanz had a shimmering pink sequinned sari throw that he kept trying to eat! Vicki measured the distance from the end of the throws to the ponies' fetlocks. She was pleased because all the girls had made their ponies' costumes a nice safe length without any dangerous dangly bits that would trip them up in the ring.

"OK, now I'll show you how to make a big knot in a pony's mane," Vicki said. Using patient little Taffy, she knotted his mane between his ears, then pinned the unicorn horn onto the bumpy knot. "That'll stay on all day, no matter how much you gallop," she said.

Cara grinned shyly. "I wasn't planning on too much galloping in my fairy outfit."

Jess tied a knot in Rose's silky mane too and pinned the pretty little posy crown in place. "My perfect flower pony!" she laughed.

As they stood admiring their ponies, Mr Reece-Thomas zoomed by in his huge four-wheel drive. The girls watched it nosily, hoping to get a glimpse of Camilla and Henrietta in their designer dresses but Mr Reece-Thomas drove so fast they couldn't see a thing.

"They're in a rush," said Jess.

"They've got to box the ponies for the show," Cara said.

"Lucky them – we've got to hack over," moaned Mel.

Vicki shook her head. "Don't complain – the ponies will enjoy the fresh air and they'll arrive at the show all the better for it," she said. "Just you see."

As the girls were grooming their ponies,

there was the thud of feet across the yard, and a stranger came rushing up to them. "We need your help, now," she snapped.

She was obviously hot, flustered and very cross. She was wearing a very old-fashioned blue jacket and skirt, both far too big for her. But what made her look really weird was the short, lopsided grey wig that kept falling into her eyes.

Sam was the first to realize who it was. There was no mistaking that snooty face underneath the grey hair – it was Camilla! Sam started to giggle. "It's Granny Worthington!" she whispered to her friends, who all burst out laughing.

"Don't just stand there staring like idiots," Camilla spluttered. "We need your help – the ponies won't box."

Before Jess could stop herself, she blurted out, "No wonder, with you dressed like that!"

"Has Cleopatra ever seen your outfit before?" Sam asked.

"And what *is* your outfit?" interrupted Mel.

Camilla scowled. "Well, it's not exactly what I was expecting," she said. "Mummy's stupid secretary got confused when she spoke to the costume hire company. Instead of asking for a queen's ballgown and crown, she told them I wanted to dress up as the Queen. When Mummy went to pick it up this morning, this it what they gave her and she couldn't change it at such short notice."

The girls were still having difficulty controlling their giggles.

"Oh, be quiet, it's not *that* funny!" shouted Camilla. "Anyway," she said, looking them up and down, "you should be pleased that there's at least one classy person in the competition. Now come and help me."

The girls looked at each other and shook their heads. They'd taken Vicki's advice and spent time making sure their ponies knew what they looked like in their fancy dress costumes. Selfish Henrietta and Camilla obviously hadn't been bothered whether their ponies freaked out on the day of the show or not.

"Come and help or we'll be late for the show," Camilla said sharply.

As the girls followed her across the yard, Mel scowled. "I don't know why she has to be so rude when she wants our help," she muttered. "Who does she think she is?"

Sam winked at her. "The Queen," She laughed. "Don't worry, at least we'll get a sneak preview of Snooty Knickers in her designer dress," she giggled.

When they saw Henrietta, the girls couldn't believe their eyes. She was covered from head to toe in rustling green paper money.

"Don't stare at me like I'm a freak!" Henrietta snapped.

Jess covered her mouth with a hand to hide her smile. "It's . . . er, unusual," she said.

Henrietta tossed her expensively cut blonde bob. "It wasn't quite what I was expecting but the designer thought it would be cool to make me look a million dollars – literally," she said.

Mr Reece-Thomas loomed up with a scowl on his fat red face. "Mmm, it cost nearly a million dollars," he grumbled.

Henrietta threw him a dirty look. "Stop complaining, Daddy. It'll be worth every penny when I win the competition," she snapped. She turned to the girls. "I can't box President because he keeps trying to eat my dress, and Camilla can't get near Cleopatra in her outfit so you'll just have to do the job for us," she said snootily. "That's what you're here for, after all."

The girls wanted to give her a mouthful but they knew Mr Reece-Thomas would only report them to Vicki.

"Chop-chop," said Henrietta. "Who's on livery duty this week?"

Sam stepped forward. "It's me and Amber this week," she said.

"So where is she?" asked Henrietta, looking round.

"She broke her arm, remember?" Sam told her crossly.

"Oh yes," said Henrietta. "She really needs

to learn how to behave around ponies. They can be dangerous if you don't handle them right."

Mel clenched her fists and stepped forward, looking daggers, but Cara held her back.

"Perhaps you'd be better looking after President yourself then," suggested Sam, "if you don't think we know how to handle him."

"Don't be ridiculous," snapped Henrietta. "It's *your* job, and I can't do it today."

"Oh yes, I forgot," said Sam, "you're busy looking a million dollars," and all the stable girls tried hard not to laugh.

With the tension broken, Sam's friends helped her with President and Cleopatra. With a lot of gentle persuasion they managed to box the two spooked-out ponies, who whinnied nervously as Jess and Mel closed the rear doors.

"I hope they'll be all right," said Jess anxiously.

Mr Reece-Thomas didn't have the manners to reply to her. He and the two snooty girls drove away towing the horsebox without even thanking the girls who had given them a hand.

Chapter 6

After grooming the ponies until their coats shone, the girls oiled their hooves. Sam pulled a face as she dabbed a brush into a tin of hoof oil. "I'll never feel the same about this stuff again," she said to Darcy, who was carefully painting oil onto Duke's neat little feet.

"What did you do with the ruined clown costume?" Darcy asked.

"After we got back from the hospital

Mum dumped it straight in the bin. I felt really sorry for her. All that work and effort she put into it. My brother Alfie said he'd smack Snooty Knickers next time he saw her!" Sam said with a laugh.

Jess looked up from plaiting Rose's silvery mane. "We'd all like to smack her," she said.

Sam stooped to paint oil on Beanz's hooves and the frisky pony immediately started to chew her spiky ginger hair. "Pack it in, Beanz!" she said sharply.

Hearing the firm tone in her voice, Beanz stopped bothering her, but then he turned his attention to nibbling Taffy.

"You're a little trouble maker." Cara was trying to tack up Taffy, but she had a soft spot for cheeky Beanz.

Mel looked up from grooming Candy and giggled. "Didn't Henrietta look awful in her million-dollar dress?" she said.

Sam grinned. "I hope it doesn't turn windy or the whole lot could blow away!" she joked.

Vicki interrupted them. "I'm just leaving for the show, girls, but I've packed your costumes into the back of my Jeep. See you over there," she said.

The girls waved her off, then quickly mounted up. Sensing their excitement, the ponies started to toss their heads.

Sam patted Beanz, who was impatiently chomping at his bit.

"OK, boy, let's get this fancy dress show on the road!" she laughed.

Vicki was right – it was good to hack over to the show. The day was hot but there was a cool breeze, which kept the ponies nice and fresh.

"The last thing we want is to arrive at the show all hot and sweaty," said Jess.

Once they'd got off the busy main road, the girls could relax a bit and let the ponies enjoy themselves. The sight of an empty bridle path sent Candy crazy.

"I'd better let her canter before she rips my arms out of their sockets," laughed Mel.

As Candy took off, Beanz whinnied excitedly.

"OK, boy, let's go!" said Sam.

She loosened her reins and Beanz broke into a canter as he tried to catch up with Candy. But no pony in the yard could outrun her. Rose, Duke and Taffy followed at a steady canter and they all came to a halt by a five-bar gate at the end of the track. Although she was really strong, Mel was having trouble holding back the feisty little Arab.

"She'd jump the gate if she had her way," she said.

Beanz tossed his head and champed on his bit. "I think he wants to do that all over again," panted Sam, completely out of breath.

Jess smiled as she stroked Rose's heaving flanks. "Vicki always says there's nothing like a gallop to blow the cobwebs away!" she said.

Cara smiled, breathless with excitement. "It nearly blew *me* away!" she gasped.

The girls settled their ponies down for the last bit of the ride, which took them along another main road. When they got to the show, Cara was amazed by the number of horse boxes parked up. "I didn't think there'd be so many people here," she said nervously.

Jess smiled and patted her friend's arm. "Don't start worrying, Car – they're not all doing the fancy dress show," she reassured her. The first people they saw and recognized were Sam's mum and her brother, Alfie, who'd been helping unload the girls' costumes from the back of Vicki's Jeep.

"Where's Henrietta Snooty Knickers?"

Alfie yelled when he saw Sam.

The other girls burst out laughing.

"I hope everybody heard that!" said Darcy.

"Wait till you see her outfit," said Sam. "You'll laugh your head off, Alf."

They tied their ponies up to a fence beside Vicki's Jeep. Sam's mum and Mel's dad were parked close by, which was handy as they'd brought lots of food and drink for the girls. Mel found the cans of drink and handed them to her friends.

Sam drank hers almost in one gulp. "I'm well thirsty," she gasped, then started to hiccup really loudly. "Oh, no, I hope these stop soon. A burping Indian princess — very classy . . . not!" she giggled.

At two o'clock some of the events started in different parts of the showground. Luckily the fancy dress competition didn't begin till three, so the girls had plenty of time to have a look round the show and then dress themselves and the ponies in their costumes. By two-thirty Cara's and Darcy's mums were settled in the spectators' seats. Jess's mum couldn't make it as she was on the day shift at the supermarket and wasn't allowed to leave early.

Everyone could see that Jess was pretty disappointed. Darcy put her arm round her. "We'll take loads of photos so you can show your mum," she promised.

The only people who still hadn't turned up were Amber and her mum.

"I hope she's OK," Sam worried. "Maybe she's had to go back to hospital."

"I should think they'll turn up at the last minute so that Amber doesn't get too tired," Vicki said.

Vicki and Sam's mum helped the girls change into their costumes. It was funny getting undressed out in the open. Shy

Cara refused to put on her tutu in front of everybody.

"You can change in my car," Vicki suggested.

Cara slid into the back seat and closed the door, then wriggled into her tights and tutu. "That was a tight squeeze," she giggled when she got out again.

Vicki helped the girls put the throws over their ponies, but nobody could stop Beanz

from nibbling the sequins on his pink sari. Sam gave him mints from the palm of her hand to take his mind off being naughty. "Silly boy – the inside of your tummy will be blinged up with sequins!" she joked.

Finally the girls and their ponies were dressed. Jess looked stunning in her gorgeous bridal dress and veil, her pretty grey pony garlanded with flowers. Cowgirl Mel looked brilliant on Candy, who tossed her long silky chestnut mane and pawed the ground as if she was a rodeo pony! Taffy, with the unicorn horn sitting on top of his creamy blond head, was the cutest sight, and Darcy in her blue Alice in Wonderland dress and long lacy bloomers looked lovely on sleek-coated Duke!

Astride Beanz with her sequinned sari, Sam looked amazing. Her mum spread the sari out over Beanz's back so that it looked like a long glittering train. The other girls

gasped when they saw the silver chains and charms twisted round Beanz's bridle.

"You look so pretty!" said Mel.

Sam grinned. "I feel like a real princess!" she said.

Just before the show started Vicki dashed up with a big smile on her face. "She's here – Amber's arrived!" she cried.

"Where is she?" Jess asked excitedly.

"I reserved a place for her in the front row so you'll see her when you trot into the show ring," Vicki replied.

The girls beamed at each other, then Sam said what they were all thinking: "Let's do it for Amber, guys!"

As the girls entered the ring, they all waved and blew a kiss to Amber, who was sitting with her mum on the front row. She looked pale and her left arm was in a sling, but with her good arm she waved and blew kisses back to her friends.

"You all look wicked – good luck!" she yelled.

The two judges asked the twenty contestants to walk their ponies round the ring so that they could inspect each of them in turn. It was only when they were walking round that the girls saw Henrietta on President and Camilla on Cleopatra. They were both having trouble with their ponies.

It was obvious that President hated the crackling paper so near to his sensitive ears, and Camilla was having trouble staying in her saddle in her tight skirt.

The other riders in the competition had all tried hard with their costumes. There was a Snow White (which made Jess pleased she'd changed her mind), an Aladdin and even a Charlie Chaplin with a bowler hat! The judges spent a long time examining not only the riders' costumes but the ponies too. There was a gorgeous little Shetland pony dressed as Dumbo the elephant, who made

everybody laugh, and a shaggy Dales pony covered in black silk wearing a witch's hat. Sam's favourite was a little boy dressed as Harry Potter: his little Welsh pony had a toy owl perched on top of its head. But the contestant who made everybody laugh was Henrietta. A little girl pointed at her and giggled.

"Oooh, look at that girl all covered in money!" she shrieked. "Can I borrow some for an ice cream?"

Henrietta shot her a filthy look, then tried to ignore her, but that didn't bother the little girl at all.

It caught Alfie's attention though. "Oi, Snooty Knickers," he shouted loudly. "I'll have some cash too. I hear there's a big bottle of hoof oil and a clown costume that need replacing."

Henrietta looked at the floor and said nothing.

"Funny," Alfie carried on, "you don't look so pleased with yourself now."

His mum, Ruth, decided it was time to shut her son up. "Come on now, Alf, I think you've made your point. Henrietta doesn't look too happy at all now."

"Good!" said Alfie.

Henrietta's face was set like concrete as she paraded round the ring. Camilla rode behind her, gripping her reins tightly as she struggled to pull down her tight skirt.

The spectators clapped as Jess and Rose passed by; they liked Mel's outfit too, and Candy really showed off by prancing daintily on her neat little feet. Cara blushed shyly with embarrassment as she was applauded, but Taffy tossed his head and showed off his fine unicorn horn, making the crowd clap even louder. The spectators loved Darcy's charming Alice in Wonderland outfit but there was no doubt who was the favourite . . .

Sam and Beanz stole all the attention. Beanz just couldn't get enough of it! But instead of being his usual silly frisky self, he walked along smoothly so that Sam's sari stayed in place across his back. He proudly shook his long silky mane and held his head high, as if he really was carrying a beautiful Indian princess.

The judges asked the competitors to
line up so they could inspect them more
closely. It was hard keeping the ponies under
control, especially Candy, but Mel gathered
in her reins and talked gently to calm
her down. The judges spent a lot of time
examining Henrietta's paper costume – one
of them even chuckled when he saw it close

up. Henrietta turned bright red with temper but she didn't let rip like she normally would have done, just in case she was disqualified.

Finally the judges made their announcement through a microphone that boomed all over the show ground.

"The winner is . . ." one of the judges started.

Amber crossed the fingers of her good hand and whispered under her breath, "Please let it be one of my friends."

" . . . for the best fancy dress costume . . . Sam Spencer on Beanz!" the judge boomed through the microphone.

Sam let out a whoop of joy that made Beanz shy. His sequinned throw caught the sunlight, making him look more stunning than ever. Sam gasped and gripped his mane tightly – the last thing she needed was to fall off just as she was announced the winner!

Sam was concentrating so hard on Beanz that she didn't notice how annoyed Henrietta looked, but her friends saw.

"Look at Henrietta's moody face," Mel whispered.

Jess, Cara and Darcy smiled at each other.

"She looks like she's swallowed a lemon!" giggled Jess.

The judge carried on with his announcement. "I don't think I've ever seen such a funny costume. The prize for the funniest outfit has to go to Henrietta Reece-Thomas on President," he boomed through the microphone.

Camilla smiled at her friend. "Well done, Hen," she said.

Henrietta gave her a dirty look. "Shut up! The last thing I want is the *funny* prize," she snarled.

"Will the two winners please come forward to collect their prizes?" the judge called out.

Beaming Sam and scowling Henrietta trotted up to the table where the silver trophies were out on show. Amber couldn't clap but she waved and smiled as Sam trotted by. Sam and Henrietta dismounted to receive their prizes and then the official photographer asked them to stand beside the judges, holding onto their ponies. As the photographer fiddled around, trying them in different poses, President curiously sniffed the paper dress that had been bothering him all afternoon.

Unnoticed, he nibbled some of the paper notes at the back of Henrietta's dress. Then a few more.

As the photographer lined up the group, President decided he quite liked the taste of the paper money and took a really big bite out of Henrietta's costume. But this time he snapped the cord that was holding the skirt together. As the photographer called out, "Smile please!" Henrietta's skirt dropped to her feet and she stood before the crowd holding her trophy just wearing her knickers!

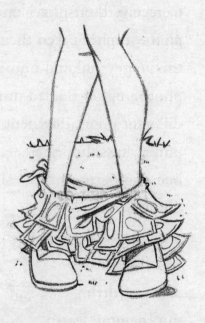

After the show Vida drove Amber back to the yard so that she could see Stella, who'd been left on her own all day. Amber leaned over the gate to the pony meadow and stroked the Highland pony with the white blaze.

"I'm sorry, babe," she murmured. "I'm not going to be able to ride you for a bit." Stella nuzzled Amber's arm, then blew into her long dark silky hair. "I'll come and see you every day though, and as soon as my cast comes off we'll go for a long ride in the sunshine," Amber promised.

After giving Stella an apple and two mints, she hurried back to the stables, where her friends were grooming down their happy but tired ponies. Sam was still as high as a kite.

"I've never won anything in my life, not even a raffle!" she said as she kissed Beanz on the nose for the hundredth time! "I couldn't have done it without my handsome boy!"

When Sam saw Amber she ran up to her and gave her a hug.

Amber winced. "Oooh! Watch my arm," she gasped.

"Sorry, but you're the nicest, kindest friend in the world," Sam told her.

Amber smiled. "I'm just dead glad it all worked out," she said.

The other girls crowded round her.

"It didn't work out for Henrietta," giggled Mel.

Jess shook her head. "I couldn't believe my eyes when her skirt fell down!" she chuckled.

"I would've died if that had happened to me," said Cara, who went pink with embarrassment every time she thought about it.

Amber grinned wickedly, and with her good hand she opened her mobile phone. "I got it on camera," she announced. She pressed a button and up flashed a photograph of Henrietta Snooty Knickers in only her knickers.

Sam burst out laughing. "That's definitely one for the family album!" she giggled.

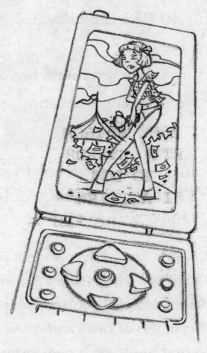

THE END

Pony Club Weekend

Pony Club Weekend

"Life has to go on. You've got to start living. That's what Dad would have wanted."

Cara and the girls are taking part in a pony club weekend at Vicki's Riding School. For her friends, camping out, showjumping and competing in lots of races sound like fun. But this is the first time Cara's been away from her mum since her dad died and she's nervous about performing in front of everybody.

Will the weekend be as much fun as they hope? And will Cara get over her fears and enjoy it after all?